Isabella Kelly

A Collection of Poems and Fables

Isabella Kelly

A Collection of Poems and Fables

ISBN/EAN: 9783744773959

Printed in Europe, USA, Canada, Australia, Japan

Cover: Foto ©Andreas Hilbeck / pixelio.de

More available books at **www.hansebooks.com**

A

COLLECTION

OF

POEMS AND FABLES,

BY

Mrs. ISABELLA KELLY.

LONDON:

PRINTED FOR W. RICHARDSON, ROYAL EXCHANGE;
J. DEBRETT, PICCADILLY; AND J. BALFOUR,
EDINBURGH.

1794.

THE writer of these verses is aware, that when works are offered in a printed form to the public, the authors must lay their account with receiving the wreath, or enduring the rod, from the hand of Criticism : and although the sanguine partiality of a parent for its offspring scarcely affords her any expectation of being honoured with the former, she indulges a hope that the circumstances under which they have come forth will exempt her from the latter, and procure her an amnesty for the many defects which she is free to confess may be found in them.

Several of the pieces were written before she had yet reached her fourteenth year ; and the rest under the pressure of a variety of domestic calamities, and the appropriate feelings of a child, a wife, and a mother ; for a father injured

jured and oppreſſed by the unfeeling hand of Power, a huſband neglected by thoſe on whom he had hereditary claims of protection, and a beloved child untimely ſnatched away: moſt of them, ſhe owns, are founded on circumſtances merely perſonal, and can therefore be but little underſtood by any but the parties concerned.— Why then (it may be aſked) offer them to the public?—To this queſtion ſhe will give an anſwer, which has, at leaſt, truth to recommend it:—Inclined by nature, and conſtrained by ſentiments of gratitude, to yield to the wiſhes of her friends, ſhe has publiſhed them ſolely at their deſire, and has choſen rather to run the hazard of Criticiſm, with all its terrors, than refuſe to her friends that compliance to which their kindneſs and good offices ſo well entitle them.

NAMES

NAMES OF SUBSCRIBERS.

A

Duchefs Dowager of Athol.
—— Alexander, Efq;
Mifs Alexander,
Mifs C. Alexander,
Mifs I. Alexander,
} Bath.

Mrs. Armitage, Chelfea.
Whalley Armitage, Efq;
Major Arnott, Marines, Fifefhire,—2 copies.
Capt. Arbuthnot, Edinburgh.

B.

Wm. Balfour, Efq; Edinburgh.
——— Buchanan, Efq; ditto.
Mrs. Brown, George-fquare, ditto.
Wm. Bolderftone, Efq; ditto.
Doctor Barton, Salifbury.
Mr. Barmley.
Mr. Beffel.
Mr. Bradbury.
Mifs A. M. Baker, Streatham.
Mr. John Brown.
Mr. Samuel Burnett, No. 26, Ironmonger-lane.
Mr. Brymer, Queen-ftreet,—4 copies.
Mr. Brand, No. 21, Princefs-ftreet.
Lieut.-Col. Barclay, Marines, Plymouth.
Ja. Bartholomew, Efq; Fifefhire.

C.

Earl of Crawford, Edinburgh,—4 copies.
Rev. Mr. Church.
Rev. Mr. T. Cook.
Mrs. Chippendal, Queen-ftreet.
Mr. Chafe, Kenfington.
D. Campbell, Efq; Sloan-ftreet,—4 copies.
Mr. Codd, War-Office,—4 copies.
Lieut.-Col. J. Campbell, Marines, Plymouth,—2 copies.
Lieut.-Col. D. Campbell, ditto, Chatham,—2 copies.
Mrs. Chriftie, Pall-Mall,—2 copies.

3

Mr. G. Coombe, Admiralty.
Mrs. Colstein,—4 copies.
Judge Cruckshan, Dublin,—4 copies.
Mrs. Chichester, Caverleigh, near Teverhan, Devon.
Mrs. Cole.
Charles Clayfield, Esq;—4 copies.
Andrew Clinton, Esq;

D.

Right Hon. Lady Harriot Don,—2 copies, } Berwickshire.
Sir Alexander Don, Bart.
Mrs. M. Douglas, No. 85, High-street, Marybone,—2 copies.
Mrs. Douglas, } Weymouth.
Miss Douglas, }
Miss Dillon, Dublin,—4 copies.
Mr. T. Dods.
Peter Dunbar, Esq; Doctors-Commons.
Miss Davidson, Glass-house-street, Golden-square.
Mrs. Deane, Bath.
Lieut.-Col. Duval, Marines, Plymouth,—2 copies.

E.

Capt. Edwards, Museum Tavern.
Eyre Evans, Esq; Dublin.

F.

Gideon Fournur, Esq; F. R. S.
Mr. John Fordyce, Clement's-lane,—4 copies.
Rev. Doctor Fordyce,—2 copies.
Miss Fordyce, Edinburgh.
Mr. Fenlayson, Museum Tavern.

G.

Right Hon. Lord Adam Gordon, Edinburgh.
Mr. Charles Grant,—4 copies.
Mr. J. Gray Gerrard, No. 47, Basinghall-street,—4 copies.
John Graham, Esq;
Lieut. Gordon, Marines, Plymouth.
Mr. Galimore, Richmond-hill.

H.

Right Hon. Lord Hawke.
Right Hon. Lady Hawke.
Capt. Hunt, Marines, Plymouth.
James Hacy, Esq; Bemerside, Berwickshire.
John Horne, Esq; Basendian.
Mrs. Buchan Hepburn, Edinburgh,—2 copies.
Mrs. Hepburn, Sloane-street.
Miss Hepburn, Campbell's-close, Edinburgh.
Miss Hepburn, Humby.

Mr. Howarth.
Mrs. Helm, Kenfington.
Mrs. Haiftwell, Richmond-green.
Mifs Hargood, Rochefter.
Doctor Holman.
George Home, Efq; Edinburgh.

I.

Colonel Innes, Marines, Portfmouth,—2 copies.
Henry Jones, Efq; New Inn,—4 copies.
Mrs. Jones, Pill, Monmouthfhire.
Mrs. Jeffries, Bath,—4 copies.
Mrs. James, Somerfet-ftreet.

K.

Lieut. Kingfman, Marines, Plymouth.

L.

Mrs. Lawrence, Portman-ftreet.
Herman Leece, Efq;
Alexander Law, Efq; Edinburgh.
John Loyd, Efq; Dublin.
Mr. James Lyon, Jamaica Coffee-houfe,—2 copies.

M.

Capt. Mackay, Royal Navy, Edinburgh.
Lieut.-Col. Macdonald, Marines,—2 copies
Mrs. Mackintofh, Kenfington.
Mr. Hugh Macklenaith, Chatham-yard.
Mrs. Mackbraith, ditto.
Rev. Mr. Morgan, Abergavenny.
Mrs. Morgan, ditto.
D. Morice, Efq; Aberdeen,—2 copies.
Mr. Maynard.

N.

Peter Nouaelle, junior, Efq;—4 copies.

O.

Rear Admiral Onflow, Poftdown, near Portfmouth.
Edward O'Shaugnefiy, Efq; Dublin.

P.

Lieut.-Col. Percival, Marines, Plymouth.
Lieut.-Col. Prefton, ditto, Valleyfield, Fifefhire,—2 copies.
Mifs A. Prefton,   ditto,   ditto.
Mifs C. Prefton,   ditto,   ditto.
Charles Plonderleath, Efq;
Lieut. Pownall, Marines, Plymouth.

R.

Mrs. Rofs, Weymouth,—4 copies.
Mrs. Cockburn Rofs,   ditto.

T. Cockburn Rofs, Edinburgh,—4 copies.
Mifs Rofs, ditto.
Mrs. Redward, Weymouth.
Lieut.-Col. Robertfon, North-ftreet, Weftminfter.
Mr. Edward Rogers, Walfham Lee Willows, Suffolk.
———— Ruffel, Efq;

S.

Mr. Severn, Queen-ftreet,—2 copies.
Mrs. Stothert of Curgen,—2 copies, Dumfries.
James Stark, Efq; Edinburgh.
Colonel Souher, Marines, Plymouth,—2 copies.
Rev. William Souter, ditto.
Mifs Charlotte Swinton, Sloan-ftreet.
Mr. Simpfon, Portland-place.
Mifs Simpfon, ditto.
Mrs. Stokes, Kenfington.
Mrs. Soilieux, ditto.
Mifs Soudon, Bath.
Meffrs. Shilly and Ravard, ditto.
Mr. D. Sandeman, No. 17, London-ftreet,—4 copies.
Mr. Sanderfon, No. 9, Glafs-houfe-ftreet, Golden-fquare,
Mrs. Sanderfon, Fulmen, Bucks.
Rev. Mr. Sanders, Ufk.
Mrs. Shaw, Dublin.
Mifs Stackpole, ditto.
Lieut. Stump, Marines, Plymouth.
Mathew Sandilands, Efq;

T.

Mr. J. Thomfon, Clement's-lane,—4 copies.
Mr. Tennant,—2 copies.
Mr. John Tracy, Brompton.
Richard Tyfon, Efq; Bath.
Doctor Robert Thornton, Charing-crofs.
Mifs Todd, George-fquare, Edinburgh.

W.

Lord Wigton, Portland-place.
Capt. Waring.
Wm. Ad. Williams, Pen-park, Monmouthfhire.
Rev. John Williams, ditto.
Mifs Winthrop, King's-road, Gray's-inn.
Capt. Henry Weir, Marines, Plymouth.
Mr. Wright, Wallbrook.
Mr. Watts, New Broad-ftreet.
Wm. Wait, Efq;
Dr. Watkins, junior, Newport, Monmouthfhire.

A COLLECTION

A

COLELCTION

OF

POEMS AND FABLES,

BY

Mrs. ISABELLA KELLY.

———————

TO THE MEMORY OF

THE LAMENTED

Mr. ROBERT HAWKE K---Y.

FAIR breaks the morn o'er yonder eaftern fkies,
And bright'ning hills in pleafing profpect rife;
But who can fay, ferene the day will end,
The fun unclouded to its depth defcend?
Such dear departed infant was thy dawn,
But gloom o'erfhades the eve my hopes had drawn.
Oh, thou! fo late my child—my hope and pride,
Who ever pleas'd, until the hour thou died,
In mournful ftrains let now my fad heart tell,
How I my darling boy could bid farewel!
Angelic brightnefs! oh! look down and fee
What bitter pangs thy parent feels for thee!

B   If

If thy pure ſhade can know what paſſes here,
Accept the burſting ſigh—the guſhing tear ;—
And thou, ſo ſoon enthron'd in realms above,
Forgive the murmurs of maternal love !
Severely kind was that all-ſacred day,
When thy ſweet form did ev'ry pain repay :
Thy angel beauty did my hope engage,
That thou ſhouldſt bleſs my life, and chear my age ;
And thou, fair ſpirit, now remov'd from pain,
Haſt taught my humble heart, that life is vain :
Yet, what is this that ſtruggles at my breaſt
For thee, my child ?—it will not be ſuppreſt :
Thy ſpotleſs innocence—thy ſoul ſo pure,
From ſcorn could not thy guiltleſs clay ſecure.
What tho' diſtinguiſh'd by *that* honor'd name
Which gain'd to Britain glory, wealth and fame,
That ſwift deſtruction o'er her foes has hurl'd,
And liv'd the pride of an admiring world ;
What tho' deſcended from that ſoldier's breaſt,
Who reigns * a hero, worſhipt in the Eaſt,
Whoſe gallant deeds adorn Indoſtan's page,
And thou the lateſt darling of his age ;
Did it avail thee, honor, worth, and grace,
Gave brilliant luſtre to thy mother's race,—

---

* Col. K——y was then living, high in reputation as in rank—
commanding the centre army in the Carnatic.

A

A noble race, where all the virtues glow,
Adorn'd with all that monarchs can beſtow ?
Ah, no! tho' thus diſtinguiſh'd by thy birth,
Thou waſt deny'd a little ſpot of earth ;
Tho' ſoft humanity exalts her creſt,
And in Britannia reigns an honor'd gueſt,
Yet cruel C--b--w-l refus'd a grave *,
The laſt retreat thy lovely form could crave
But if unhallow'd was thy cloſing ſcene,
Thou angel innocent art now ſerene ;
And tho' no coſtly marble e'er may grace
Thy low-repoſing bed—thy reſting-place—
Yet ſhall the faireſt flowers the ſpot adorn,
Cheriſh'd with pureſt tears of early morn ;
And angels guard thy guiltleſs ſleeping clay,
Till thou awakeſt to eternal day.
How ſweet *thy* reſt ! from ev'ry evil free !
" The world is left to wretchedneſs and me."
Oh, why !—but ſoft—be ſtill, my murm'ring breaſt,—
My little angel's gone to endleſs reſt ;
With kindred ſpirits, far remote from pain,
He waits the hour when we ſhall meet again.

---

* Neither clergyman nor ſexton were in the church-yard—and
the corps obliged to be carried back till next day.

To the MEMORY of ELIZA F-----E

AN EXEMPLARY MOTHER.

IF worth departed e'er deferv'd a tear,
Sacred to merit, pay the tribute here;
Repos'd beneath, to rife to life again,
Unfpotted worth, which never knew a ftain,
A tender mother, and a virtuous wife,
A noble patern of unfullied life;
Honor'd in age, lov'd and admir'd in youth,
Here reft in peace thy piety and truth.
The Chriftian virtues in her bofom reign'd,
The poor and friendlefs were by her maintain'd;
The widow bleft her charitable dome,
And wand'ring orphans found a fhelt'ring home;
More than her little pow'r allow'd, fhe gave,
Nor ever knew *that* virtue how to *fave*;
The bright example of a virtuous mind,
Is all the dow'r this parent left behind;
Few were her comforts in this varying ftate,
A painful pilgrimage her weary fate;
Few were her joys on earth while doom'd to dwell,
So fmiling died, and foftly faid, " I'm well."
Fair fainted fhade ! forgive this ftarting tear,
A haplefs daughter ftill would wifh thee here,

But

But heaven, more juſt, more gracious, deem'd it hard,
That worth like thine ſhould wait a late reward,
So gently mov'd thee to that peaceful ſhore,
Where pleaſure reigns, and anguiſh is no more.
Sweet be thy reſt, dear venerated clay!
Whoſe guardian care once watch'd my erring way;
Ere thy pure ſpirit gain'd its native ſkies,
Thou taught'ſt each fair idea how to riſe;
Supremely bleſt thy mourning daughter, *I*,
By thee taught how to live, and how to die;
And by thine own example, ſhew'd the way,
That leads to peace, and never-ending day.
Still deign to guide me, ever-honor'd ſhade!
In that clear path thy ſhining virtues made;
O thou! ſo tried in ſad affliction's ſchool,
That made the Chriſtian Leader's life thy rule.
Oh, while I live may I diſtinguiſh'd be,
By ſtill revering, imitating thee!
Serene with kindred ſaints in pureſt air,
Now ſmile in triumph at thy late deſpair.

The CHOICE; *or,* DULL HOUR PAST.

HEIGHO! I'm wond'rous dull; in truth I'm wond'rous
    ſad—
Little amuſement, and the weather bad;

What

What shall I do? I'l' write—Come, ready friend—
I mean my pen—Good folks, I pray attend:
Still at a lofs, I do not wifh to teaze ;—
My mufe, affift me—teach me how to pleafe—
My thoughts are free—then, fancy, take thy range—
I'll write my wifh—no choice—pfhaw, how I change!
Critics, be dumb—I will the thought impart,
That fome kind youth may bid for Anna's heart:
He who afpires this little heart to gain,
Some decent fhare of merit mult attain ;
Serene religion muft his actions guide,
Bright truth, nice honor, o'er his mind prefide ;
Prudence to guide him thro' life's bufy fcene,
Never extravagant, nor ever mean ;
Let him have fenfe defigning men to fee,
Enough to rule himfelf, and *govern me* ;
To feel for human kind—a generous foul,
To me devoted, but polite to all ;
His temper kind—of that I muft be fure—
A hufband's frown I never could endure ;
To female weaknefs mild reproof impart,
But with indifference never chill the heart ;
No *foolifh* fondnefs fhould he ever fhew,
But love refin'd, within his bofom glow ;
His manner eafy, gen'rous, void of art,
Let ev'ry word flow candid from the heart ;
His perfon pleafing, in his tafte refin'd,
A face the index of an honeft mind ;

T

To jealousy he never must give way,
Trust to my honour, and I'll not betray;
No flatt'ring fribble shall my hand obtain,
Where much is said, there little can remain;
A man for riches I can never prize,—
Let kindness grant what adverse fate denies;
I wish not wealth, nor titles do I claim,
Only let goodness mark his honest name;
To little errors I will kindly bend;
His wish, my law, I never will contend;
And, should he stray (as none can faultless be)
Prudence shall veil it; for *I will not see:*
A youth like this to share the cares of life,
Shall find in me a kind and faithful wife.
Ambitious females in their wealth may glee,—
Love, worth, and honor, form the heart for me.
Methinks ye frown—I hear ye loud exclaim,
" To hope so much a female is to blame;
" In modern days, do you expect to find
" Grace, worth, and goodness, with firm honor join'd ?
" But if so high are your pretensions, tell
" What do you boast ? in what do you excel ?"
In great sincerity I now step forth,
Confess my merit humble as my worth;
I boast no beauty—I no graces claim,
And all my portion is, a spotless name;
Sincere and artless—MAN exert your skill,
With prudent fondness make me what you will.

Blushing

Blushing, methinks, I hear it said, " No more !
" No other claim !—truly your merit's *poor*."
Yet, in life's varying maze, I hope to meet
Some kindred heart, unpractis'd in deceit.
To prove the tender friend—companion—wife,
Will be the sweetest care of Anna's life ;
With temper mild, and innocently gay,
Submissive gentleness she'll ever pay.—
My friends, adieu !—my hour is past away.

MIRANDA *and the* RED-BREAST :

A FABLE FOR THE LADIES.

THE vain Miranda long had shone,
   In fashion's brilliant scene ;
Each heart confest her passing fair,
   And hail'd her beauty's queen.

Unrival'd long Miranda liv'd,
   Of British maids the toast,
And with tyrannic sway she reign'd,
   A celebrated toast ;

Till brighter Emeline appear'd,
 Fair as the opening morn,
Then Myra only fwell'd the groupe
 Sweet Emma did adorn.

The haughty maid, that ne'er could brook
 Ev'n one neglecting eye,
With burfting pride beheld her charms
 Unnotic'd now paft by.

Conflicting paffions tear her breaft;
 To diftant fcenes fhe flies,
To feek in folitude that calm
 Reflection ne'er denies;

But ah! in vain, the venom'd dart
 Within her bofom lay,
And pride repreft can ne'er beftow,
 Of peace the fainteft ray.

One filent eve fhe reach'd a grove,
 There to lament her fate,
Where modeft Robin penfive fung,
 And chear'd his little mate:

With fcorn fhe heard the plaintive lay,
 And, with difdainful look,

" Prefuming feeble wretch," fhe cried;
  The little redbreaft fhook:

" Chirp not, thou vain, thou forry thing,
  " Hark Philomela's ftrain;
  Unworthy thou to fhare her haunts,
  " The meaneft of her train:

" Be ever dumb, affuming bird,
  " Dar'ft thou e'er hope to pleafe,
" When larks falute the early morn,
  " And thrufhes fing from trees?

" Ambitious thing, I fay give o'er;
  " The blackbird's warbling fong
" In juft contempt will fink thy notes;
  " For ever ftop thy tongue."

Meek Robin, in the fweeteft ftrain,
  With fofteft accents fpoke,
Shelt'ring his partner with his wings,
  Thus, trembling, filence broke:

" Pardon, bright fair! I know not pride,
  " Foe to ambition I;
" Humbly poor Robin owns he ne'er
  " With thrufh or lark can vie:

Indeed

" Indeed I try to imitate
    " Sweet Philomela's lay,
" And to the warbling blackbird's fong
    " Sincereft homage pay;

" And when that wintry ftorms defcend,
    " Each vernal beauty feize,
" When they retire till milder hours,
    " Poor Robin tries to pleafe;

" 'Tis then with timid hope I ftrive
    " To foothe the liftening ear,
" My bright reward, a little food,
    " Thefe hours of want to chear:

" Then hear, ye fweeteft birds of air,
    " The humbleft of your throng;
" 'Tis when ye will not deign to chear,
    " Poor Robin gives his fong:

" Hence learn, Miranda, bright and fair,
    " Let meeknefs pride difarm;
" Vouchfafe to learn from little me,
    " Heaven gives to each a charm."

To hear a moral from a bird,
    Abafh'd Miranda ftood,
Return'd to town, fought Emeline,
    Was happy, kind, and good.

THE

THE REFORMED MAN OF FASHION,
TO HIS FRIEND.

BLEST under that domeſtic roof
   I once contemptuous view'd,
When gay and thoughtleſs like thyſelf,
   I varied bliſs purſued.

The modeſt manſion, woods, and ſtreams,
   Could then no peace afford
To that loſt heart which borrow'd hope
   From " ſeven's the main, my Lord."

Reflection then was death to me,
   In vain I ſigh'd for reſt ;
It fled the diſſipated ſcene,
   And the polluted breaſt ;

Deep ſunk in faſhion's giddy round,
   Far loſt in folly's maze,
When a kind parent's anxious care
   Reform'd my erring ways ;

The ſilent tear of fond regret
   Stood trembling in his eye ;
His meek, his unreproving voice
   Sunk in the pitying ſigh,

                        Awoke

Awoke that dormant filial fpark
    Which ftill inform'd my foul,
Soften'd that proud, ungovern'd heart
    Which never brook'd controul;

Led by his kind directing hand,
    I turn'd from error's way,
And fought thofe guiltlefs, happy fcenes,
    From which I ne'er can ftray;

For charming Anna met my glance,
    Confefs'd a mutual flame,
Accepted vows which bleft a heart
    With all a heart could claim.

In her foft breaft, where virtue dwelt,
    Where confcious honour fhone,
I view'd the bleffings of a life,
    The contraft to my own.

So pure her life, fo fair her truth,
    To *think*, her fweet employ;
To view the *paft*, brought fmiling peace,
    The *future*, hope and joy:

And now reflection chears my foul,
    And at the clofe of day,

                          When

When confcience ev'ry deed approves,
    Emits a brighter ray."

Come then, my friend, and kindly fhare
    Our peaceful, frugal fare;
'Twill foothe thy forrowing heart to view
    The pleafures dwelling here.

Meek mercy keeps our humble gate,
    The welcome's modeft want;
The poor and friendlefs blefs the mite
    Our little ftore can grant.

Far from ambition's fhrine we live,
    Remote from pride and ftate;
Our harmlefs wifhes Heaven grants,
    And chears our humble fate.

From happinefs then who would rove, .
    Poffefs'd of all that's fair?
For I can call my home an heav'n,
    An angel dwelling there;

A little fmiling, prattling race,
    Juft opening into day;
Their mother's purity and worth
    Their infant charms difplay;

To deck their minds with modeſt worth,
   Which time and death defies,
To guide the ſlippery paths of youth,
   And train them for the ſkies.

This is my Anna's chief delight,
   This is my glad employ;
Her lovely daughters claim her care,
   And mine my blooming boy.

Our hours by bounteous Heaven thus bleſt,
   We, at the cloſe of day,
With love, with gratitude, and truth,
   United homage pay.

To ARTHUR.

Go, artleſs lay, and if thou canſt diſcloſe
The ſoft effuſions which this breaſt encloſe,
Go, humble lines, and tenderly impart
The deareſt wiſhes of a grateful heart;
But neither tongue nor pen can e'er reveal
The warm emotions I muſt ever feel;

                  Then

Then fancy all thy own kind lips would fay,
Think all efteem---love---gratitude can pay.
Had I the fweetnefs of an angel's tongue,
The charm of numbers, and the power of fong,
Harmonious grace fhould flow in ev'ry line,
When offering gratitude at friendfhip's fhrine ;
But fince no mufe will deign to aid this lay,
Let feeling dictate, and let truth difplay ;
Oh ! form'd with all that can the heart endear,
A temper generous, and a foul fincere,
With kind acceptance grace the offer'd line,
Where true regard and friendfhip mildly fhine ;
Then take, my Arthur, from thefe trembling hands,
The trifling tribute which thy love demands.
Aufpicious hour ! when nature fram'd thy mind
To blefs and dignify the human kind ;
Gave thee a heart to feel for others woe,
A generous tear for worth deprefs'd to flow ;
Imprefs'd thy foul with virtue's facred laws,
And firmeft honour to fupport her caufe,
Soft emanation fparkling in thine eyes,
Like thofe bright worlds that fhine in evening's fkies ;
But what *I* think thee, cannot be expreft,
My future conduct will unfold it beft ;
Each rifing morning, and each evening's clofe,
" I'll afk of Heav'n thy undifturb'd repofe,"
That peaceful fcenes thy flumbers may difplay,
And joy falute thee each returning day,

And

And fhould again thy country claim thine arm,
To guard our rights, or fhield our land from harm,
Amid the din of war, and martial ftrife,
I'd foothe the dangers of my foldier's life ;
With all the foftnefs in a female's power,
Beguile the languor of each painful hour ;
No frown fhould cloud my brow, I'd happy be,
Nay feel it pleafure, being fhared with thee ;
Or fhould (which Heaven avert) fome fated blow
Come arm'd with power to lay my Arthur low,
Fate would be kind to guide me to my reft,
My deareft home, my foldier's faithful breaft,
To clafp his fainting form, clofe his dead eye,
Blefs his lov'd name, and breathe my lateft figh :
Ne'er e'en in death my Arthur I'll refign,
Be all his fufferings, all his forrows mine ;
But fhould fome fweet retirement be thy fate,
Far from ambition's path, far from the great,
To humble fhades contented I'll defcend,
With thee, my hufband, my protecting friend ;
The chearful day ferenely will I fit,
Learn from thy goodnefs, and admire thy wit ;
Whilft I delighted in my bleft employ,
(For hours of innocence are hours of joy)
And when the evening warns thee to thy reft,
Peaceful repofe upon thy faithful breaft :
Thus rich in innocence, fecure from wrong,
We'll blefs the moments as they glide along ;

The

The bleft above will view our peaceful fate,
And fmile to fee an emblem of their ftate;
Be this our meed, kind fovereign of the fky!
We'll live in innocence, in triumph die.
" All-giving Power!" great fountain of reward,
From perfect blifs Oh! deign me thy regard;
And if fuch worth can need my humble prayer,
Oh! make my Arthur thy diftinguifh'd care;
Let thy good angels all his fteps await,
And fhield his bofom from the ftorms of fate;
Around his couch let nightly guardians 'tend,
And from each unfeen ill my love defend!
But in this erring, ever varying fcene,
Should darker clouds o'erfhade our ftate ferene,
Oh! thou great Power, omnipotent and wife!
Teach us thou fendeft bleffings in difguife;
And when arrives that laft important hour
When every pleafure lofes every power,
When the laft fpark of vital fpirit fails,
And peaceful confcience over death prevails,
Thou beft of Beings! all our fteps uphold,
To fmooth the paffage heavenly fcenes unfold,
And fafely bear our fainted fpirits high,
To fome bright manfion in our native fky:
Thus may our guiltlefs pleafures ever bloom,
And rife fuperior o'er the filent tomb.

To

TO THE MEMORY OF THE LATE
CAPTAIN T. H. ABBOTT. *
RESPECTFULLY ADDRESSED TO THE OFFICERS OF
THE ARTILLERY.

FROM dreary scenes low prostrate on the ground,
Where anguish rages with a gloom profound;
Where poverty in ev'ry form appears,
To chill a wretched prisoner with fears,
A spirit fled; the brave, undaunted mind
Smil'd at despair, and left its load behind;
Oh! Henry, must thou undistinguish'd lie,
Sunk, unremember'd all thy virtues die;
And will no friend whom all those virtues made,
Pay a just tribute to thy parting shade?
Yes, I'm that friend; accept the pitying tear,
The kindest offering of an heart sincere;
Oh! take it then from her you once approv'd,
The friend you honour'd, and the maid you lov'd;
Benignant shade! Oh! yet one glance bestow,
I'll guard thy memory, and indulge my woe;
How hard thy fate! from peace, from pleasure torn,
Doom'd to imprisonment, in want to mourn;

* This officer was imprisoned for money laid out on account of
Government, when he commanded in Florida. About an hour before his death an express arrived with the news of his having suc-
ceeded to 800 l. per annum.

On the damp earth expos'd, thy gallant breaſt
With ſickneſs, anguiſh, pining care oppreſt;
Too proud for pity, conſcious of the paſt,
Forgot, unheeded even to the laſt,
Thou found'ſt no friend to cloſe thy dying eye,
To anxious watch the unrepeated ſigh;
No gentle hand thy lateſt wants reliev'd,
Nor cordial drop thy cloſing lips receiv'd;
But loſt, neglected, unrewarded died,
A man in whom the virtues did reſide:
Ye brave companions of his happier days,
Oh! aid my feeble voice to ſpeak his praiſe;
He once was leader of a choſen band,
And carried conqueſt thro' a foreign land;
Lov'd by his equals, to his ſoldiers dear,
To each forgiving, to himſelf ſevere;
His mild compaſſion chear'd the wretch's fate,
But unregarded was his ſuffering fate,
Till death, more kind than country, friends, or king,
Shelter'd his ſorrows with his ſable wing:
Pardon, ye brave! long, long did ye protect
That injur'd worth his country did neglect;
Then join with me the kind embalming tear,
For Henry's fate deſerves a pang ſincere;
And may thy reſt be ſweet, thou good and brave!
Bright honor rear her ſtandard o'er thy grave;
And though no marble may adorn the ſpot,
A name ſo honor'd cannot be forgot;

Dear

Dear to the foldier, by the good approv'd,
Sacred to friends, and by relations lov'd.
And Oh! bleft fpirit! gracious and benign,
O'er all my ways Oh! let thy influence fhine:
Pure, unimpaffion'd now thy care extend,
And be my guardian, comforter, and friend:
Direct the good, the fhafts of ill repel,
Till I fhall bid each earthly blifs farewel;
Then may thy fpirit welcome mine above
To the bright regions of feraphic love.

TO AN UNBORN INFANT.

BE ftill, fweet babe, no harm fhall reach thee,
   Nor hurt thy yet unfinifh'd form;
Thy mother's frame fhall fafely guard thee
   From this bleak, this beating ftorm.

Promis'd hope! expected treafure!
   Oh! how welcome to thefe arms!
Feeble, yet they'll fondly clafp thee,
   Shield thee from the leaft alarms.

Lov'd already, little blefling,
   Kindly cherifh'd, tho' unknown,

                     Fancy

Fancy forms thee fweet and lovely,
   Emblem of the rofe unblown :

Though thy father is imprifon'd,
   Wrong'd, forgotten, robb'd of right,
I'll reprefs the rifing anguifh,
   Till thine eyes behold the light.

Start not, babe ! the hour approaches
   That prefents the gift of life ;
Soon, too foon thoul't tafte of forrow
   In thefe realms of care and ftrife :

Share not thou a mother's feelings,
   Hope vouchfafes a pitying ray ;
Tho' a gloom obfcures the morning,
   Bright may fhine the rifing day,

Live, fweet babe, to blefs thy father,
   When thy mother flumbers low ;
Softly lifp her name that lov'd him,
   Thro' a world of varied woe.

Learn, my child, the mournful ftory
   Of thy fuffering mother's life ;
Let thy father not forget her
   In a future happier wife.

                                     Babe

Babe of fondeft expectation,
    Watch his wifhes in his face ;
What pleas'd in me, mayft thou inherit,
    And fupply my vacant place.

Whifper all the anguifh'd moments
    That have wrung this anxious breaft,
Say, I liv'd to give thee being,
    And retir'd to endlefs reft.

WRITTEN IN VERY DEEP AFFLICTION.

LOW on affliction's gloomy bed,
    Where forrow holds her reign ;
Where pleafure never deigns a glance,
    I pray for peace in vain :

Far, far remote from joy, from hope,
    No foothing voice I hear ;
Nor doth fair friendfhip lend one gleam,
    My fainting heart to chear.

Ah fortune ! ever varying fhade !
    Falfe, difappointing fhrine !
To lure the young, believing heart,
    How bright thy profpects fhine !

Con-

Contentment once illum'd my breaft,
   No anxious care had I ;
Sereneft flumbers, fweeteft reft,
   With dreams of peaceful joy.

Returning morn new pleafures gave,
   I woke to foft delight;
But now my ev'ry blefling's fled,
   Day finks in horror's night.

Be ftill, fome fpirit whifpers, ceafe,
   Thy fuffering foon fhall clofe ;
I come to guide thy wandering feet
   To undifturb'd repofe.

Why ftart at death's approach,—drear fhade,
   It leads to purer air,
Immortal joys that never fade,
   No ill approaches there !

Come, fear me not ; tho' cold and pale,
   I now affert my claim :
No guilt thy finking foul alarms ;
   Why trembles then thy frame ?

But hark ! fome angel whifpers, ftay,
   Hope humbly that reward

Promis'd to purity on earth,
   From Heaven's bright regard.

Then raife thy poor dejected heart;
   Remember there's a Power
That gave thee being to be bleft,
   But wifely hides the hour:

In faith, hope, virtue, perfevere,
   Nor yield to black defpair;
For thy great Parent's arm will guide
   Each daughter of his care.

Then let thy foul fecurely reft
   On that Almighty word
That gracioufly difpenfes good,
   And comfort will afford.

E

EXTEMPORE AFTER A DISPUTE AT DUNKERQUE.

AH! why fhould paffion rend a generous breaft,
  Or tears of anguifh dim a chearing eye,
When gentle means could charm ev'n thought to reft,
  Soothe ev'ry care, reprefs each rifing figh?

Or why let cold indifference chill that blifs,
  Defign'd by Heaven to blefs the human kind,
Or bleak negleft avert the peaceful kifs,
  The fweeteft offering of a yielding mind?

Then now let love, let peace their home regain,
  And meek-eyed mercy fay, " thou art forgiven,"
And mutual o'er our ruder paffions reign,
  Until they guide us to their native Heaven.

To

To a Wandering Husband, from a Deserted Wife.

SAY, where is that charming repofe
   That fo lately illumin'd my breaft,
Like the fun that fo chearfully fhone,
   And at eve footh'd me kindly to reft ?

Alas ! it no longer is mine,
   No more on my morning it beams ;
Defpair now poffeffes its place,
   And prefides even over my dreams.

Why did my fond credulous heart
   Give delufion fuch eafy belief ;
Why liften with rapture to vows
   Now forgot, and devote me to grief?

Alas ! whenfoe'er I attempt
   A refpite from anguifh to find,
From the world and its fcorn I retire,
   Still, ftill it adheres to my mind ;

The admonifhing fpirit within
   Thy confcience muft whifper, beware !

                          Hafte

Hafte—reftore a fond wife to delight,
  A mother preferve from defpair.

The foft fouthern gale as it blows,
  Appears with my forrows to mourn ;
Gentle echo with pity replies,
  " Mary's peace ne'er again can return."

Tho' religion's meek aid I implore,
  Yet the fofteft ideas arife ;
And this heart, tho' difdain'd, ftill adores
  What my reafon no longer can prize.

But alas ! could the error be mine ?
  Say, could it e'er fpring from my mind,
When fo fondly thou often haft faid,
  Mary's bofom is chafte and refin'd ?

Still triumph—my wrongs are unknown ;
  Oh ! torture be hufh'd, be repreft ;
To be pitied I yet am too proud,
  And thy fame is ftill dear to my breaft ;

Ever dear ! yet be warn'd by my love ;
  Retribution's bright morning will rife,
And thofe wrongs, unremember'd by thee,
  Some angel will waft to the fkies.

Farewel

Farewel to each blessing below,
 My moments to care I resign;
Though I die, may thy pleasures increase!
 Thy Mary will never repine:

To the grave thy fond wife will retire,
 It will shelter—will yield her repose;
Its coldness will chill her warm heart,
 Free thee—and her sorrows compose.

EXTEMPORE *in the* GARDEN *of a* CONVENT *belonging to*
LES SOEURS NOIR, *à* BOURBURG.

HAIL blest retirement! to this calm retreat
The sorrowing wretch may turn her weary feet;
Here hopes, and fears, and wishes, sink to rest,
And, here, serene becomes the tortur'd breast;
No anxious cares can here the mind alarm,
No hope for pleasure, nor no dread of harm;

Far from temptation's wiles thefe faints refide,
Heaven their purfuit, and innocence their guide;
Wrong-judging world! that deem thefe cells the tomb,
And think thefe walls conceal defpairing gloom,
Approach and view the inmates of this place,
Their peaceful manner, tranquil, fmiling face;
Approach, and learn from thefe fo truly good,
Where Heaven refides, nor difcontents intrude,
Where true religion, unaffected truth,
The conftant guide of their unerring youth,
At length fhall lead them to the bleft abode
Of kindred faints, their Saviour and their God.

———————

TO A BROTHER, ON ENTERING THE ARMY.

ACCEPT, my Charles, from thy ftill anxious friend,
Some ufeful counfel by affection pen'd;
To my advice you oft have deference paid,
Which bids me hope this laft will be obey'd;
Nought but your good could force me to expofe
The humble talents which I now difclofe;
Then, my dear brother, kindly plead excufe
For ev'ry error of your fifter's mufe:

First,

First, my young soldier, let me recommend,
In life's fair spring to make your God your friend;
That Power you in the bloom of youth engage,
Will ne'er desert you in declining age;
In danger's hour he'll prove the truest friend,
On him for all you want and wish depend;
Unto your parents every rev'rence pay,
'Tis God's command their precepts to obey;
Be duteous, open, tender, and sincere,
Support their age, to their advice adhere!
Let strictest justice every action guide,
And truth with honor o'er your mind preside;
Be firm in friendship, scorn all mean disguise,
Nor suffer mean resentment to arise;
On your superior's favour ne'er presume,
Nor, to inferiors, haughtiness assume;
Reprove with firmness, rule with gentle sway;
Thro' love, not fear, teach soldiers to obey;
Watch o'er yourself, to them be not severe,
They then will love you, and your worth revere;
Beware of passion, it unmans the soul,
If once indulg'd, it never brooks controul;
Thro' all the varying scenes of this frail state,
'Tis temper shades the colour of our fate.
Temp'rance, dear youth, I warmly recommend,
In fumes of wine too oft is lost a friend;

Oh!

Oh ! fly the phrenzy like contempt or fcorn,
Though mad at night, reflection comes with morn :
Duels avoid, if you with honor can,
It breaks thro' laws prefcrib'd by God and man ;
Alas ! too late the deed you may repent,
Be warn'd ! the pangs of dire remorfe prevent ;
Trembling, I charge thee, fatal gaming fhun,
A dangerous vice that thoufands has undone ;
It lures the heart with fmiles, oh ! fad deceit,
And ne'er forfakes till ruin is complete.
Never be rul'd by fafhion, but by fenfe,
Neither be apt to give or take offence ;
Be not ambitious riches to attain,
For truft me wealth is not exempt from pain ;
Aim at a competence with credit bleft,
In every point we find the medium beft.
To wedlock's ftate I dare but little fay,
The youthful heart in general takes its way ;
I only raife to Hymen's throne my voice,
That he may lead you to a happy choice ;
Dear as you are, detefted be your name,
Should e'er you bring the innocent to fhame ;
E'er ftain the honor of a virtuous race,
Or bring a helplefs female to difgrace ;
Scorn to their ruin any aid to lend,
For man was born their honor to defend.
When we're apart, you on fome diftant fhore,
Remember Anna, and thefe lines read o'er ;

They

They are her counfels, breath'd with love fincere,
My only brother ! then to them adhere;
So will your conduct ftill unclouded fhine,
Your fame ftill brighten as your days decline.

EXTEMPORE ON ARRIVING IN THE COUNTRY.

CAN filent pleafures give my love the fmile
 Of fweet content, of happinefs ferene ?
Can Anna's care, her tendernefs beguile
 The languor of a folitary fcene ?

Yes, for with anxious love I'll watch his eye,
 His will, his wifhes in his features trace;
With fond impatience to prevent them fly,
 My fweet reward, a fmile from his dear face.

F   IN

'Tis thine, great Lyttelton, to raife the foul,
And every low idea to controul;
To form the manners, to enrich the mind,
To guide each paffion, and to read mankind:
The rude, the unreform'd by thee are taught
To drefs expreffion, and refine the thought;
To act with dignity, converfe with eafe,
And teach that happy art—the way to pleafe:
To human kind thy genius fure was given,
A bounteous bleffing from indulgent Heaven:
Tho' now in darknefs death thine eye hath clos'd,
Thy facred relics in yon tomb repos'd,
Enlightened ignorance fhall blefs thy name,
The yet unborn immortalize thy fame.

Lines

LINES FOR THE BLANK LEAF OF MY PRAYER BOOK:
WRITTEN ON A SUNDAY.

WHILST wanderers, deftin'd here on earth to ftray,
This facred page will point the better way;
'Twill foothe each care, 'twill chearful faith impart,
Amend each error, and direct the heart;
Teach, with fair profpects not to be elate,
Nor fainting fink beneath the frowns of fate;
Nor ever murmur at what Heaven denies,
But think each crofs a bleffing in difguife.
When pleafure's maze difplays alluring charms,
When ills and dangers fpread their dire alarms,
Thefe lines were by kind Providence defign'd
To clear illufion, and compofe the mind.
All gracious Power! vouchfafe to hear my pray'r!
Guard me, and guide me with thy kindeft care:
Each rifing morn fweet gratitude I'll pay,
For the dear bleffing of this facred day.

F 2

T.

To the Memory of the Honorable
Miss CAROLINE CAMPBEL.

HOW soft the morn ! how sweet the early day !
What blooming tints the opening clouds display !
Delusive shades ! the bleakest storms oft rise,
And cloud the brightness of the purest skies.
In blushing spring the budding leaves may fall,
And ye, you fair, receive an early call ;
Ah ! Caroline ! how promising thy bloom !
How chang'd, how sad, how sunk in sorrow's gloom !
How fair thy prospects ! charming maid, how bright,
Which death relentless veils in endless night ;
Blights those sweet hopes admiring friends had form'd,
Chill'd that soft friendship which thy bosom warm'd.
Why did not pitying powers thy virtue save,
Preserve our hopes from disappointment's grave ?
Form'd with each grace that could enrich the mind,
With wit, with sentiment, and sense refin'd ;
The gentlest soul inform'd her glowing breast,
Heaven's meekest image on her form imprest ;
The softest mercy, purity, and truth,
Adorn'd her name, gave lustre to her youth :
Heaven, that with virtue did her heart endow,
Sent her a pattern for her sex below.

Ye fair companions of her opening bloom,
Weep o'er her duft, and profit at her tomb;
She once was all the human kind adore;
" Now view her relics, and be vain no more."
What now alas! avails her noble birth,
Her eafy manners, her diftinguifh'd worth!
Silent and cold as yon pale marble buft,
Reduc'd her honors to unconfcious duft.
And fhall no more thy friends behold thy face,
No more be charm'd by thy perfuafive grace!
And fhall no more thy accents chear the maid,
Who *now* invokes thy lov'd, thy honor'd fhade?
Tranfporting hope! in realms of brighteft day, ⎫
Thy foul fhall gain that fpark, that quick'ning ray, ⎬
To wake, re-animate thy fleeping clay. ⎭
Extatic thought! in thofe bright realms above
I'll hail thy virtues with an angel's love;
When a few fleeting years fhall fet me free,
My foul, unfhackled, then fhall fly to thee;
But if on earth I longer muft refide,
Oh! then bleft Caroline be ftill my guide!
And fhould thy fpirit know what paffes here,
Oh! deign to dry the haplefs Mary's tear;
Be that, fweet maid, thy facred, foft employ,
Till fhe fhall meet thee for eternal joy.

RETIRED THOUGHTS TO A DEPARTED INFANT.

Go, firſt, ſweet hope ! to thine own Heaven ſucceed,
While here thy mother's heart muſt ever bleed,
Muſt ever mourn, till that auſpicious day
That lays me where thy much-lov'd aſhes lay.
This lonely hour my ſorrows reach no ear,
This lonely hour no eye beholds *this* tear ;
My angel ! thou from thy reſplendent throne
Oh ! take this moment, it is all thine own ;
Spite of religious aid my wiſhes riſe,
Ah ! me ! how weak to wiſh thee from the ſkies !
Sometimes (deluſion ſtrong) I ſee thee ſmile,
I hear thy liſping voice my cares beguile,
And fancy wandering (how remote from truth)
Surveys thee blooming in the pride of youth ;
Beholds thee *all* a mother can implore ;
Reaſon returns, and ſays, thou art no more !
Ah ! ſad remembrance, why exert thy power,
Why, why recal the paſt endearing hour,
When thy ſweet frame upon my breaſt repos'd,
And opening beauty every look diſclos'd ?
Each *happier mother*, vain of her delight,
Still, ſtill obtrudes her darling on my ſight ;

Then

Then in the harmlefs fmile, the feeble cry,
I hear thy voice, I fee thy languid eye :
Oh ! ftill my child, if in thy perfect ftate,
Thou haft a knowledge of *my* fuffering fate,
In gentle dreams thy beauteous form difplay,
And bring me tidings from the realms of day ;
Tell thy fad mother *when* the hour draws near,
That we fhall meet, nor other parting fear ;
And Heaven, ftill gracious to the mourning kind,
Oh ! deign to fend me peace, a will refign'd ;
Save me from murmurs at thy high decree,
And teach my heart, that's *beft* that pleafes thee.

ON THE RIGHT HONORABLE GENERAL C——Y
LOSING HIS ELECTION FOR BURY ST. EDMUND'S.

AN humble mufe prefumes thy worth to boaft,
Says D——'s conquer'd, and that C——y loft ;
Still thou doft triumph in the nobleft part,
Still doth preferve the generous patriot's heart ;
Thy principles, great Chief, exalt thy fame,
And ever fhall immortalize thy name ;
For ever lov'd, diftinguifh'd muft thou be,
For brighteft virtues ever fhone in thee ;

2   Thy

Thy noble acts are well in Britain known,
And generous friendſhip marks thee for her own ;
Then glory, C——y in this ſeeming fall,
Thou riſeſt ſtill ſuperior over all :
The day will dawn when Britain's ſons ſhall ſee
Their nobleſt privileges prized by thee ;
Thou like the ſun in yonder weſtern ſkies,
Only declin'ſt, more glorioully to riſe.

———

EPITAPH ON A FAVORITE TAME CHICKEN.

BENEATH this ſtone a chicken's laid,
   Her miſtreſs named her Beſs,
Six months ſhe tenderly was nurſed,
   Yet ſtill ſhe grew the leſs.

In fairy hill poor Beſs was hatched,
   If there ſhe had but ſtaid,
She might have had a verdant grave,
   And not in duſt been laid.

But hapleſs chick, like this world's fools,
   Muſt wander far from home,
And by a lady's ſciſſars fell,
   And here muſt fix her tomb.

                            Farewell!

Farewell! my little favourite Bess,
   Thy fate why should I mourn?
Since kings and queens the same must share,
   And unto dust return.

———————

TO THE MEMORY OF AN HONEST MAN, MR. B. D.
ADDRESSED TO HIS WIDOW.

WHEN wealthy, proud, or titled fools expire,
(Those splendid trifles which the vain admire,)
The flatterer's pen, the sculptor's curious art,
May strike the eye—but seldom reach the heart;
Tho' gaudy trappings did not grace his birth,
And undistinguished, save, by honest worth,
Tho' polished marble do'nt record his praise,
Nor humble fortune, monument can raise;
Tho' his low grave can boast no featured bust,
Celestial guardians watch his sleeping dust;
And Heaven hath spared his memory one friend,
Who knew his goodness—viewed his peaceful end;
Then thou pure spirit deign one glance to see,
How sweet the task to utter truth of thee;
And thou sad mourner, take it from my hands,
This boon thy friendship from my pen demands:

       G   Nor

Nor mourn thy want of power to fave his name,
By means, which only wealth or pride can claim,
Accufe not fate, but vanity defpife,
His humble afhes will as fafely rife,
And claim as juft a title to the fkies
As thofe whofe marbled hiftory proclaim
The ONLY TITLE they e'er had to fame.
He knew no guile, to pleafe his chief delight,
Serene his confcience—his intentions right;
His fentiments fuperior to his ftate,
Too noble minded for his lowly fate;
Since upon earth none are from error free,
Why fhould I blufh to own a fault in thee?
From prudent caution thou didft widely roam,
Nor once remembered want might vifit home;
In this wife age, well practifed how to *fave*,
Wealth will condemn what generous pity gave;
Who now will foothe thy lonely widow's care?
Give her, what oft thy little ftore did fpare.
Prefumptuous pen ! be calm foreboding mind,
Heaven will be ever bounteous, good and kind;
In Mercy's annals are his deeds enroll'd,
The FIRST OF BEINGS will reward unfold.
And now dear mourner will you condefcend
To accept this offering from a conftant friend?
Ah! ceafe to weep thy fainted partner's fate,
Who, placed above this fublunary ftate,

Muft

Muſt now condemn the tender flowing tear,
Wonder who loved ſo well, could wiſh him here ;
Or cou'd thy ſorrow, cou'd thy pining grief,
Reſtore thy huſband, or bring thee relief,
Could guſhing tears recall the ſpirit fled,
Or burſting ſighs awake the ſleeping dead ;
Or could thy mourning bring him back to woes,
Say—could thy love diſturb his ſweet repoſe ?
Ah no ! in realms of bliſs remote from pain,
He waits the hour, to re-unite again ;
But be reminded, (deem it not ſevere),
'Tis the reward of PATIENT ſuffering here ;
Farewell, my friend ! in Heaven's gracious time,
Thou'lt meet thy huſband in a purer clime ;
Where boundleſs joy awaits the truly good,
And no rude ſtorm can ever more intrude.

THE VISION.

THE moon had joined the ſplendid height,
    The world retired to reſt,
When William waked to weep the night,
    For cares diſturbed his breaſt.

Eliza's

Eliza's lofs he mourned in vain,
    For death her eyes had clofed,
Silenced that tongue which foothed his pain,
    And every grief compofed.

Oh ! baneful death he ftill would fay,
    Why did'ft thou torture me ?
My peace had never known decay,
    Fell tyrant, but for thee.

My bleft Eliza ! ftill he cries,
    Thou haft thy forfeit paid ;
When lo ! before his wandering eyes,
    Appeared the confcious fhade.

Celeftial charms adorned her face,
    The fmile of peace fhe wore ;
And whifpered with angelic grace,
    " My William mourn no more.

" Nay, ftart not love ! difpel all fear,
    " The meffenger of peace,
" I come to ftop the gufhing tear,
    " And bid thy mourning ceafe.

" Did'ft thou fuppofe relentlefs death,
    " Wou'd not his claim affert ?

" Or did'ft thou think the fleeting breath,
   " Wou'd never leave the heart ?

" Oh ! ceafe to weep, to mourn forbear,
   " From forrow I am free,
" And fmile at every earthly care,
   " Except the care of thee.

" The gentle paffion which we knew,
   " That cheers the guiltlefs mind,
" Exalted ftill I feel for you,
   " In purity refined.

" In thofe bright realms remote from woe,
   " Where funs eternal fhine,
" Imperfect blifs I only know,
   " While you for me repine.

" I did not take a long adieu,
   " Thou wilt not long feel pain,
" Thy friends muft mourn, muft weep for you,
   " And we fhall meet again.

" O'er all thy ways I kindly wait,
   " I ward each threat'ning ill ;
" I'll guide thee in this erring ftate,
   " Thy guardian angel ftill.

And

" And when thy foul is gently fled,
 " To thofe fine realms of day,
" Some guardian fpirit of the dead,
 " Shall watch thy fleeping clay.

" Thou'ft not forgot the awful hour,
 " When death affailed my heart,
" When fternly he denied the power,
 " My wifhes to impart.

" Then hear me now, protect our race,
 " 'Tis thine to guide their youth[7];
" With love like this my memory grace,
 " Let this difplay thy truth.

" But fee—the gates of light unclofe,
 " My love, a laft adieu,
" I go to undifturbed repofe,
 " There wait to welcome you.

An

ANSWER TO THE SONG OF "TRUST NOT MAN," &c.

I'LL not truſt, nor man deceive me,
　I'll elude his deepeſt art;
He ſhall wed and be deſerving,
　E're I give my much loved heart.

I don't want *thee* kind adviſer,
　Man ſhall never me perplex;
I ſhall ſtill continue prudent,
　And defy the faithleſs ſex.

I never truſt an artful ſtory,
　Ever to my heart take heed;
To me they ſhall be always humble,
　Or they never ſhall ſucceed.

Nor like a bird I'll be deluded,
　Virtue ſtill ſhall guard my heart;
'Till I find a faithful lover,
　It and I ſhall never part.

On beholding Arthur asleep.

SWEET be thy fleep my only love !
   Serene and foft thy flumbers be ;
But fhould thy fleeping fancy rove,
   Guide it ye pitying powers to me !

Difclofe my image to his view,
   This faithful bofom true and kind ;
Whifper, my prefent fmiling care,
   Can ill difplay my anxious mind.

Long may my arm fupport his head,
   Or kinder ftill this beating breaft,
His flumb'ring hours to fondly watch,
   When waking charm his foul to reft.

With filent pleafure I will wait,
   With duteous, tender care attend
Thy gentle flumbers, bufy hours,
   My guide, my love, my hufband, friend !

Ye powers ! but I may fpare the prayer,
   Such worth good angels will employ,
The fweet reflection of a life fo pure,
   Infures my Arthur dreams of peaceful joy.

Ye ever bright, celeftial fhining train,
   That guide the actions of the good and brave,
Oh deign! to aid my fond, yet feeble power,
   To blefs that life, I pray kind Heav'n to fave,

ON A CHILD'S BIRTH DAY.

SMILING bleffings, pleafures gay,
Grace fweet Shirley's natal day,
Brighten ftill her opening fcene,
Ever be the day ferene!
May each virtue grace her mind,
Her temper meek, her fenfe refined,
Be her gentle, guiltlefs breaft,
The fair abode of peace and reft!
Innocence her fteps await,
And fhield her from the ftorms of fate;
Virtue be her darling pride,
And guardian angels be her guide;
May kind Heaven's protecting power,
Shield her to her lateft hour!
Deign to aid a parent's care,
To make her good as fhe is fair!
And may fweet Shirley ftill inherit,
Her mother's virtues, father's fpirit!

H

To

[50]

To the Memory of Lieut. James Abernethie, Lost on board the Glorieux, 1782.

EACH weeping mufe affift my mournful pen,
To praife a foldier, and lament a friend;
Loft to the world in life's gay early bloom,
The clouds his mourners, and the deep his tomb;
No gentle friend received his parting breath,
No friend to foothe the bitter hour of death;
Tho' dreadful waves, and high tempeft'ous wind
Raged round his head, yet he was calm within:
For he was pure as is the mountain fnow,
Mild as the fouthern breezes when they blow;
His early virtues blafted in their prime,
The blooming youth was loft at twenty-nine;
Ye unavailing tears forbear to flow,
I'll fay what truth doth to his memory owe.
Born with a noble, with a generous heart,
He knew no wifh but what he might impart:
A friend fincere, his parent's hope and pride,
His brother's comfort and his fifter's guide;
Each manly virtue graced the gentle youth,
" The foul of innocence, and pride of truth."
Worth, honour, candour, were in him combin'd,
An angel's form, but more angelic mind;
With generous love his youthful bofom glow'd,
With generous fentiments his heart o'erflow'd:

And

And tho' he slumbers in his wat'ry tomb,
His memory will to lateft ages bloom:
To youth furviving he hath left behind,
The bright example of a fpotlefs mind;
Thou dear departed friend a long farewell!
Upon thy worth my thoughts fhall ever dwell;
Still to thy fhade fweet youth I'll drop a tear,
And ever mourn thee, with a heart fincere;
E'er yet I clofe, bleft fhade! if in thy power,
My guardian be, in each eventful hour,
From thy bright realms oh! kindly condefcend,
To guard thy faithful, thy lamenting friend,
Still watchful of thy charge, bleft fpirit be!
For fuch an office I'd have done for thee;
That ftation keep, until I reach that fhore,
Where we fhall meet, and death can part no more.

REFLECTIONS AFTER VIEWING A SCENE OF DISTRESS.

TEACH me, all gracious Power, to be content!
   To blefs my lot becaufe ordained by thee;
Ne'er mourn for that, thy wifdom hath not lent,
   But deem it good becaufe thy great decree.

Then ceafe vain heart to mourn the want of power,
    Juft Heaven will view, accept the willing mind;
Will give reward in retribution's hour,
    To all who felt the ills of human kind.

What tho' I can't beftow the wifh'd fupply,
    Nor cheer cold poverty's obfcure abode;
Ne'er read the language of a grateful eye,
    Nor guide the helplefs penitent to God.

I often wifh the uninformed to teach,
    To give to orphan infancy its bread,
To foothe the forrow of declining age,
    And give THAT *pittance* which *I yet* may need.

Be hufhed complaint—be never murmured more,
    Arraign not that great plan to Heaven known;
Perhaps endowed with fplendour, wealth and power,
    The kinder feelings had not been my own.

With pleafure circled, proved fecure from fear,
    Perhaps I ne'er had breathed a pitying figh;
Might never offered others woes a tear,
    But lived a ftranger to each fofter tie.

Then 'tis in mercy wealth hath been denied,
    For now—a foul that feels for all is mine,

I yet

I yet can foothe the ills of fuffering worth,
　And pray the bad their purpofe to refign.

And I can cheer the modeft with applaufe,
　Kindly fupport the weak, the forrowing mind,
Can plead, unblufhing, virtue's injured caufe,
　Conceal the failings of my erring kind.

The voice attuned to foftnefs may reprefs
　The anguifhed figh—relieve the doubting heart,
A pitying look will often foften pain,
　A MITE to penury will joy impart.

A friendly fmile can welcome modeft fear,
　A chearful word beguile the gloom of age ;
Hence then defpondency—hence difcontent,
　I ftill have worth which partial friends engage.

Yes—thefe are mine, and thefe the good approve,
　Moft gracious power ! that all thofe gifts beftow,
In mercy, ftill withhold the means of ill,
　And let me all unto thy mercy owe.

Then while on earth I'll thy great name adore,
　And fink with fweet compofure to the duft !
Blefs thy paft mercies—" humbly hope for more,"
　From thee my GOD, PROTECTOR, GVIDE and TRUST.

T

THE HAWK, THE MAGPIES, AND THE PIGEONS.

A Fable, very respectfully addressed to the Hon. Mrs.
E—tw—k.

TRUTH oft in fables is convey'd,
And morals too in tales display'd;
And what discretion won't exprefs,
Fiction may veil in pleasing drefs;
Thus I, when prudence dare not plead,
I make a bird my fermon read.
Ye who the modest highly prize
Attend a Pigeon in disguise,
And learn each chatterer to despife;
For ah! too oft the chattering tongue,
The heart of innocence hath ftung;
And had the hero of my tale,
Permitted flander to prevail,
A helplefs, difappointed pair,
Had now been victims of defpair.
Some years ago a hawk expired,
Dreaded by foes, by friends admired;
To gain Britannia's deathlefs fame,
And immortalize his own great name,
Glory he made his early aim;
He lived unequalled, died revered,
To every bird was Hawk endeared;

He left a son, his deareſt care,
His hope, his bleſſing, honour's heir:
In him each milder virtue ſhone,
For goodneſs marked him for her own;
His kindneſs friendleſs birds redreſt,
His ſheltering wings the orphan bleſt;
To ſay the whole, his worth maintain'd,
The glorious name his ſire had gained.
This noble Hawk to moſt endear'd,
Beneath his wing a pigeon rear'd:
From India's clime to Britain's ſhade,
The infant ſtranger was convey'd,
To early learn that genuine worth,
Which ſhould diſtinguiſh birds of birth;
Hawk " *took it up a little flower,*"
And placed it in a kindly bower,
Saved him from each inclement ſtorm,
His tender years ſecured from harm,
His infant mind with virtue dreſt,
A bright example taught the reſt;
Thus happy, honoured, much improved,
Our Pigeon lived by Hawk beloved;
But when the years of reaſon came,
(Alas! what age ſecure from blame?)
Love triumphed, and he took a wife,
More dear than liberty or life;
The worthy Hawk in wonder loſt,
Perceived his views, his wiſhes croſt;

Yet ſtill beſtowed his guardian care,
And ſmiled delighted on the pair;
The Pigeons thoughtleſs, gay and young,
Believed each ſmoothe, betraying tongue;
They truſted hope, they baniſhed fear,
Nor ever dream't a danger near,
'Till indiſcretion's train advance,
The effects of vain extravagance:
Behold them then, to want expoſed,
Each error heightened—then diſcloſed;
Regretted follies, bitter thought,
The leſſon of experience taught.
Their ſoft complaints, their burſting ſighs,
The tears that trembled in their eyes,
The Hawk with pitying glance ſurvey'd,
And ſent the mourners liberal aid.
Far from his heart, though near his neſt,
There lived a race to birds a peſt;
The magpies named, a chattering crew,
On miſchief bent, about they flew;
The worthy held them in diſdain,
Hawk ſpurn'd them from his honeſt train;
But though they ne'er approach'd his ear,
They ſtill contrived that he ſhould hear,
Each folly of the humble pair,
Theſe favor'd pigeons of his care;
They tried in vain with varied art,
To rouſe ſome paſſion—turn his heart;

Cries

Cries one— " it moves me even to rage,
" That Pigeons fhould a Hawk engage !
" How better deck'd his board had been,
" Had he thefe pigeons never feen ;
" His plumage ftill had been more gay,
" But for the gold he gives away ;
" This, Hawks may think benevolence,
" But Magpies deem it want of fenfe."
" Not too fevere," a fage one cries,
" The virtues of a Hawk I prize ;
" Wou'd he the voice of prudence hear,
" So good a bird we muft revere ;
" Or wou'd he liften to *our tale*,
" Permit his reafon to prevail,
" And let his gold diftinguifh *worth*,
" His favour grace a Magpie's birth ;
" With gratitude our breafts fhould glow,
" What praifes fhould our tongues beftow !
" But ah ! my friends we fpeak in vain,
" He ever treats *us* with difdain ;
" The Pigeons faults will ne'er appear,
" He blots each folly with a tear."
" But," adds another, " fting his pride,
" Say Hawks and Pigeons are allied ;
" To prove they have not any claim,
" (For they muft fuffer all the blame),
" He'll ne'er again their faces fee,
" Which may make room for thee or me."

I

But

But oh! they little knew his mind
Was generous, noble, good and kind;
It forrowed for the poor accufed,
To hear their pleading ne'er refufed;
And with great fentiments infpired,
He reafoned thus at eve retired:
" 'Tis true the Pigeons may be wrong,
" But I'll not truft a magpie's tongue;
" All that e'er breathed to error's prone,
" In pitying theirs I veil my own;
" An unforgiving heart fhould be,
" Itfelf from imperfection free;
" Then mercy for the pair fhall plead,
" T'will fhield myfelf in hours of need;
" The days of youth are full of harm,
" Each pleafure wears a tempting charm;
" And when it can old birds allure,
" How can young Pigeons be fecure?
" And if to give deferves fuch praife,
" Such feelings to the heart conveys,
" How bleffed every mite that's given,
" So honoured *here*, approved by Heaven!
" What pleafure in an added difh,
" Or robe I neither want or wifh;
" Or where the merit to beftow,
" *That* which brings joy they ne'er can know;
" Then I refolve the pigeon pair,
" Shall ftill my kind protection fhare."

He

He then retired to peaceful reft,
With an approving confcience bleft;
Oh may his reafoning ftill impart,
A leffon to the human heart!
And thou bright fair! whofe worth, and truth,
So lately bleft a favoured youth,
And thou oh! E—tw—k fo elate,
How kind thy ftars, how bleft thy fate;
That gave thee in the fpring of life,
The accomplifhed friend, the charming wife;
Accept the offering of a breaft,
With warmeft gratitude impreft;
And oh! vouchfafe, bleft pair to hear,
The wifhes of a foul fincere;
Long may ye bloom, and fee each grace,
Reflected in a lovely race!
And as too often cares intrude,
On the kind bofoms of the good,
May fweet domeftic peace beguile,
And make the face of forrow fmile!
And when that love no more can warm,
Efteem fhall lend a milder charm;
Enliven'd friendfhip ftill engage,
And cheer the wintry hours of age;
Long may ye live in joy to fee,
An offspring from each error free;
And in the lengthen'd honoured line,
A H——ke's diftinguifhed virtues fhine!

THE

THE EAGLE, THE KITE, AND THE COCK.

An Emblematic Fable, most respectfully addressed to the Right Hon. General C——y. Written in the year 1788.

IN former days when birds could speak,
And held their courts three times a week,
Nay, had their councils—held debate—
Had Lords and Commons, Church and State;
With gentle sway an Eagle reign'd,
His charity the poor maintained;
So mild—benignant—that his mind,
To heaven-born clemency inclined;
Mercy and justice prop'd his throne,
His deeds are through Britannia known;
But to sum up this Eagle's praise,
Our Royal George his worth displays;
But as the best of Eagles may
By evil birds be led astray,
He placed his confidence—delight,
In a dissembling, cruel Kite;
From *Hatfield's* woods the tyrant came,
Nay, Hatfield still can tell *his name;*
The generous heart is soon deceived,
The Kite professed, his King believed;
And fatal tarnish to his reign,
He named the Kite, L—d C——b——n;

* It is not to be supposed this alludes to the present most noble Marquis of S———y.

I   Then

Then all that had a claim, or right,
Muft pay obeifance to this Kite;
But to pourtray his wily deeds,
Attend the *fact* that now fucceeds:
In Eagle's court there dwelt a Cock,
That rear'd a numerous happy flock;
For nineteen chicks his dame did brink,
Fifteen he meant to ferve their King;
And gentle partlets worth and grace,
Adorned the little guiltlefs race;
This Cock the Eagle's fire had ferved,
And of the fon had much deferved;
He fought their battles, fpilt his blood,
Yet to his poft he firmly ftood;
But when returned, he deemed it hard,
Never to fhare the leaft reward;
But with his partlet meek and kind,
In fad obfcurity he pined;
To raife their pretty helplefs flock,
Solely employed the valiant Cock;
'Till chance his piteous tale conveyed,
To charming R—l—y's peaceful fhade;
Where dwelt a bird of noble race,
His mind was fraught with every grace,
His heart to worthieft deeds inclined,
He felt the woes of all his kind;
And acting for the general good,
Refolved to quit his favourite wood;

The

The wider to extend his fway,
To Eagle's Court he winged his way;
To blefs a nation's ample round,
The monarch's confidence he found;
When near the throne, in power high,
He viewed our Cock with pitying eye;
His Godlike mind, on bleffing bent,
A gracious mandate quickly fent;
And thus our injur'd bird addrefs'd :
" Thy wrongs by me fhall be redrefs'd;
" Repair with fpeed to Eagle's court,
" My intereft fhall thy caufe fupport."
The Cock obey'd, his grateful brood,
With tears of joy his hands bedew'd.
Behold him placed to ferve his King,
Beneath the fhade of C——y's wing;
His heart was loyal, actions pure,
Poor bird ! he deem'd his blifs fecure;
His partlet happy, chickens good,
He hoped no griefs would e'er intrude;
But ah ! how blind to human fate !
Between the ins and outs of ftate
There rofe, alas ! a ftern debate.
How fatal to our Cock's repofe,
'Twas then his baleful planet rofe;
His noble patron—guardian friend,
No longer would at court attend.
The Eagle cried (his friends then few)
" And wilt thou leave me, H——d, too?"

}

He look'd, he figh'd, to Eagle bow'd,
(The fofteft thoughts his memory croud)
" I've ferv'd thee long, my gracious Sire,
" My honor bids me now retire ;
" I cannot league with thofe that fawn,
" H——d's retirement marks their dawn ;
" Thy name I blefs, thy worth revere,
" Nought but my confcience half fo dear.
" Beloved Liege ! thefe truths receive,
" And now with prayers I take my leave."
'Twas then the Lords, with courtly grace,
Tried to fucceed to H——d's place ;
Though many tried, not one could boaft
Thofe charms the King in H——d loft ;
At length the Kite the Eagle pleas'd,
And fwift the envied ftation feiz'd ;
His fpecious manner, artful fmile,
The unfufpecting foon beguile.
The Cock, not loweft in his train,
Wifhes his friendfhip to obtain ;
For his dear chicks (even birds afpire)
He wifh'd to rife a little higher ;
With winning grace the artful Kite,
Promis'd to aid the foldier's right ;
He faid, " a council fits on high,
" I'll bear thy wifhes to the fky ;
" Eagle will ne'er reject thy prayer,
" Soldiers are children of his care ;

" I'll

" I'll bring his gracious pleasure down,
" And may succefs my efforts crown!"
The Cock he crows—with hope elate,
In triumph views his future fate ;
To partlet and her groupe he flies ;
" My love, my dearest chicks, he cries,
" The generous Kite fupports my claim,
" Be ever bleft his honor'd name !"
Meek partlet weeps—the chickens dance,
And think in life they'll have a chance :
Ah ! blind to fate ! the ftorm impends,
That blights thy hopes, deftroys thy friends ;
The gloomy power from ebon throne
That birds and beafts, even man muft own,
Aim'd at poor partlet's breaft a blow
That laid her and her wifhes low :
The widow'd Cock reclin'd his head :
Deprefs'd with forrow, reafon fled ;
His chicks exert their fofteft powers,
To foothe their parent's languid hours ;
But all their filial duty fail'd,
His wild delirium ftill prevail'd ;
A doctor then, with folemn face,
Declar'd the Cock's a doubtful cafe ;
And to the C-----b-----n did fend
His oath, that he could not attend :
'Twas in that fad, that anguifh'd hour,
The Kite exerted cruel power ;

The

The loyal Cock next day difgraced,
Another in his room was placed;
And birds there were (perhaps too bold)
Declar'd, Lord Kite the place had fold;
Mean time the Cock held lingering ftrife
Between the powers of death and life;
And when returning reafon came,
Remembrance faint, he could not name
The Kite, but cried, " my chickens dear,
" He is my friend, I need not fear;
" For your dear fakes I'll life endure;
" While I exift, your bread's fecure;
" Ye are too young your food to gain,
" Or ftorms of winter to fuftain;
" And more—without a father's care,
" What will not *birds of prey* oft d re !"
Languid and weak, no more he faid,
But meek reclin'd his drooping head;
Fondly then view'd his children near,
And foon difcern'd the ftarting tear;
For long his chicks their grief repreft,
At length itb urft their fuffering breaft;
That cruel Kite, detefted name !
I fad him depriv'd of bread and fame;
He trembled, look'd, his heart grew fick,
Yet thus addrefs'd his eldeft chick :
" Sweet emblem of my partlet's worth,
" Child of my love from early birth,

K

" Thy widow'd parent's fate behold,
" *Now* loft, expos'd to want and cold,
" The victim of contempt and fcorn,
" Of treachery too ; ah me forlorn !
" Survey thefe chicks of tender age ;
" Let thefe thy every power engage ;
" Go feek the Kite, o'er him prevail,
" The plea of innocence can't fail ;
" He will not *perfevere* in wrong,
" But liften to thy guiltlefs tongue ;
" Exert thyfelf, a parent's need
" Will teach a daughter how to plead."
The chick replied, her tears fuppreft,
While varied paffions tear her breaft,
" Beloved parent ! fwift I go :"
She ftopt—her tears began to flow :
Then wildly to the Kite fhe flies,
With drooping wings and languid eyes ;
The ferving birds, in order ranged,
Believ'd the chicken much deranged ;
Denied her entrance—faid that he
Would never any ftranger fee :
She gasp'd for breath, fhe tried to fpeak,
She look'd—yet ftill the look was meek ;
Her meeknefs pleas'd—her looks prevail,
For when did ever meeknefs fail ?
They let the little chicken in,
And thus the trembler did begin :

" Pardon

" Pardon, great Lord ! nor think me rude ;
" For mercy—juftice—I intrude ;
" The daughter of the injur'd Cock ;
" I come from him—from all his flock ;
" Low at thy feet a victim fee ;
" She prays for him that trufted thee :
" Be gracious then—the Cock reftore ;
" Indeed I never begg'd before ;
" Let mercy plead—fome pity lend
" To one who never could offend !"
Proud of his ftate, the Kite look'd down
With a malignant, fcornful frown ;
Saying, " thy race I do not know,
" Nor could I deign to be thy foe ;
" But thou the Cock, I think, didft name ;
" I recollect—he merits blame :
" Prefuming thing ! I fay begone ;
" Thy father's arts are not unknown ;
" Dare he e'er hope for my fupport,
" That for his poft did gold extort
" From my brave major—worthy friend ?
" And yet the Cock did ne'er offend !
" The King the fhameful deed fhall know ;
" Go home, rafh chick, and tell him fo."
    [Ere I proceed, I muft premife,
(My tale would fuffer from difguife)
The bird, the Kite alluded to,
Was a poor, lazy, dull cuckoo ;

That

That, like his race, to birds a peſt,
Crept meanly to another's neſt;
But ſtill he could not but allow,
And on his honour muſt avow,
His patron's falſehood to defy,
And accuſation to deny;
For that, ſo far from giving gold,
He hever did the Cock behold;
Nay, wrote for every bird to view,
The Cock he never even knew.
Benignant reader! I digreſs;
Pardon: I will no more tranſgreſs.]
   With honeſt pride, indignant eyes,
The aſtoniſh'd chick with firmneſs cries,
" My father's fame ſhall brightly ſhine
" When ſhame ſhall cover thee and thine;
" Even now, deteſted tyrant, now,
" They curſe thy deeds that lowly bow;
" And learn, proud Lord, tho' greatly placed,
" With ſe.ming honor highly graced;
" A juſt, a gracious Power reigns,
" That falſehood even in Lords diſdains;
" In *retribution's awful hour*
" Thou't feel that vengeful Being's power;
" He'll aim at thy baſe heart a blow,
" With kindred fiends, to lay thee low;

                       " Nor

" Nor hope for mercy—never pray ;
" Juſtice o'er thee preſides *that day* ;
" But ſhouldſt thou dare—remember'd be,
" Almighty Powers ! his deeds to me.
" My parent pray'd---he was abuſed ;
" I kneel for mercy---am refuſed :
" Adieu, thou baſe, deſtructive Kite !"
Thus ſaid, ſhe took an inſtant flight.
I'll veil her meeting with the Cock,
The mutual tears of all the flock ;
Oh ! wou'd I alſo cou'd conceal
Thoſe ills each honeſt bird muſt feel ;
The gallant Cock, to griefs a prey,
The varied ills of power diſplay,
Expos'd to forrow, want, and debt,
With duns and poverty beſet,
Each morn he wakes to guiltleſs fear,
No friend to aid, no hope to cheer ;
The pledges of his much-lov'd wife,
More dear to him than fame or life,
Scatter'd, neglected, hopeleſs driven,
By bleakeſt blaſts of angry Heaven,
To ſeek beneath an humble ſhed ;
To ſhield the weary, languid head,
And gain the hard-earn'd daily bread ;
Their beauteous plumage all deranged,
Their virtues hid, their friends eſtranged ;

They

They pine---they mourn---but do not live;
Can righteous Heaven the Kite forgive?
Daughters and fons of human kind,
Whom bright benevolence doth bind,
Accept this fable; it conveys
A fact which real life difplays,
A mournful truth of courtly ways;
It reprefents a foldier's fate,
Sinking beneath oppreffion's weight;
His claims rejected---robb'd of bread,
Without a home to fhield his head
From the rude world's inclement ftorms,
From poverty in direft forms;
His children fcatter'd and diftrefs'd,
Their worth neglected---hopes deprefs'd;
To honor born---in affluence bred,
Behold them now---each bleffing fled:
They cannot beg----a noble race
Remember'd, flufh the pallid face;
They every fentiment refine,
And, victims of regret, they pine;
The fole diftinction they can boaft,
Is, that they have not virtue loft.
Ye Great! in fortune's favour high,
Vouchfafe to bend a pitying eye!
Should e'er this family be known,
Or on your goodnefs e'er be thrown,

Be kind---protect a parent's age,
In his defence, ye good, engage!
Survey his mild perfuading form,
And fave his guiltlefs groupe from harm.
Ye highly placed, fupreme in power,
Should ye e'er find a vacant hour,
Oh! deign this little tale to read,
Your hearts will for a foldier plead;
And *thou* of adamantine foul,
Whom *juftice* never could controul,
Shouldft thou this little fable fcan,
And confcience cry " THOU ART THE MAN,"
Receive the warning offer'd here,
A daughter pleads, and Heaven will hear:
But thou to whom *thefe lines* I fend,
Thou *firft* of mortals---firmeft friend,
Thefe fad, fad truths fo often heared,
Thy heart hath pitied---bounty cheared;
Thy mercy was the kindly ray,
The ftar that chear'd the gloomy way;
Still deign thy gracious aid to lend,
Thy powerful influence extend;
Supported by thy liberal hand,
Thefe lines will all I wifh command:
Oh! thou lov'd excellence revered,
So honor'd, and where known endeared;

Long

Long may thy virtues mend the mind,
And blefs the hours, of human kind;
Then, when this dream of life is o'er,
Thy fame fhall bloom for ever more,
And gratitude with pride proclaim
The worth that graced a C------y's name.

FINIS.

www.ingramcontent.com/pod-product-compliance
Lightning Source LLC
Chambersburg PA
CBHW022010050726
47499CB00008BA/2825